J. Hewitt

The Fairy Bridal. A Cantata

Anatiposi

J. Hewitt

The Fairy Bridal. A Cantata

Reprint of the original, first published in 1871.

1st Edition 2023 | ISBN: 978-3-38217-396-8

Anatiposi Verlag is an imprint of Outlook Verlagsgesellschaft mbH.

Verlag (Publisher): Outlook Verlag GmbH, Zeilweg 44, 60439 Frankfurt, Deutschland
Vertretungsberechtigt (Authorized to represent): E. Roepke, Zeilweg 44, 60439 Frankfurt, Deutschland
Druck (Print): Books on Demand GmbH, In de Tarpen 42, 22848 Norderstedt, Deutschland

THE

FAIRY BRIDAL.

A

CANTATA

BY

J. H. HEWITT.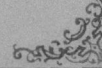

Subject founded on Shakspeare's "Mid-summer Night's Dream."

BOSTON:

OLIVER DITSON COMPANY.

NEW YORK: CHICAGO: PHILADELPHIA: BOSTON:
C. H. Ditson & Co.   Lyon & Healy   J. E. Ditson & Co.   John C. Haynes & Co.

THE
FAIRY BRIDAL.
A
CANTATA
BY
J. H. HEWITT.

Subject founded on Shakspeare's "Mid-summer Night's Dream."

BOSTON:
OLIVER DITSON COMPANY.

| NEW YORK: | CHICAGO: | PHILADELPHIA: | BOSTON: |
| C. H. Ditson & Co. | Lyon & Healy. | J. E. Ditson & Co. | John C. Haynes & Co. |

48 4

DIRECTIONS.

The Cantata of the "Fairy Bridal" was originally composed for a class of young ladies, and consequently confined to two parts, viz. soprano and alto voices. Even thus cramped, it met with much favor. The author, however, desirous that it should throw off its juvenile character, made an accompaniment of *bass* and *tenor;* simple, it is true, yet presenting a fuller harmony.

Of course the teacher will use his own judgment in the selection of voices to compass the various parts; but it is suggested that, as *Titania's* music ranges, in some instances, full two octaves, a mezzo soprano of a bold and brilliant quality should be selected. Should the cantata be needed for a Female Seminary, where bass or tenor voices cannot be procured, the part of *Oberon* may be taken by a good *alto*, and *Puck* likewise. The *bass* of the pianist or director may be used in all the choruses. It is particularly needed in the solo of the *Storm Spirit.*

The stage should be decorated with evergreens, representing a fairy grove and grotto as nearly as possible. The dresses should be characteristic, particularly those of *Night, Aurora*, the *Gnomes*, and the *Water Fairies*, the latter being composed of the most juvenile portion of the class.

The *Chorus* should enter during the introduction preceding the first chorus; the other characters at their proper periods.

CHARACTERS REPRESENTED.

Titania, Soprano. *Oberon*, Tenor or Alto. *Puck*, Bass or Alto. *Gnome King*, Bass or Alto. *Moonshine*, Soprano. *Peachblossom*, Alto. *Sunbeam*, Soprano. *Ripple*, Soprano. *Starlight*, Alto. *Dewdrop*, Soprano. *Zephyr*, Soprano. *Three Fairies of the Mist*, 1st and 2nd Soprano and Alto. *Storm Spirit*, Bass.

Speaking characters, *Night, Aurora* and *Water Fairy.*

THE FAIRY BRIDAL.

Scene represents a grove and grotto with a flowery bank. Stage dark. Soft organ or melodeon music. NIGHT *enters, clothed in a black dress, studded with stars.*

NIGHT.
Awake, ye sleepers! Lo! the rosy streak
That hangs upon Aurora's youthful cheek.
The cricket's song no longer greets the ear
Of the dull owlet. See, night's dewy tear
Hangs on the cowslip, panting for the sun,
That gives new life to all he shines upon.
Ye winged Fays that dwell in flow'rets' cup,
And, like the bee, drink its heart's nectar up,
Come forth! Ye gnomes, from caverns damp,
Where burns for aye the mystic meteor lamp,
Awake! come forth! while sombre Night retires,
And, one by one, puts out the heavenly fires.

Your Fairy Queen to-day resigns her hand
To Oberon, the proudest of the Fairy-land.

AURORA *enters opposite.* (*Gas turned on.*)

AURORA.
Back, gloomy Night! put out each twinkling light!
Aurora rises o'er the mountain height,
Decked in her robes of gold and crimson hue,
While the proud sun peers up the dome of blue,
And gladdens nature, giving life to all
That shrank beneath thy cold and sable pall.
Back to thy cave! Aurora bright appears,
And sips from every flower night's dewy tears.

(*They retire.*)

INTRODUCTION.
Con furia.

No. 1.

Chorus enters while the introduction is going on.
Allegretto.

Awake, awake, awake, awake! Awake, awake, awake!

1. Ye fays that love the si-lent dell, And in the cup of flow'ret dwell; Ye spir-its of the moonlight lawn, Who
2. The light is creeping up the sky, The owl has closed his wea-ry eye; The whippoorwill has hushed its tune, And

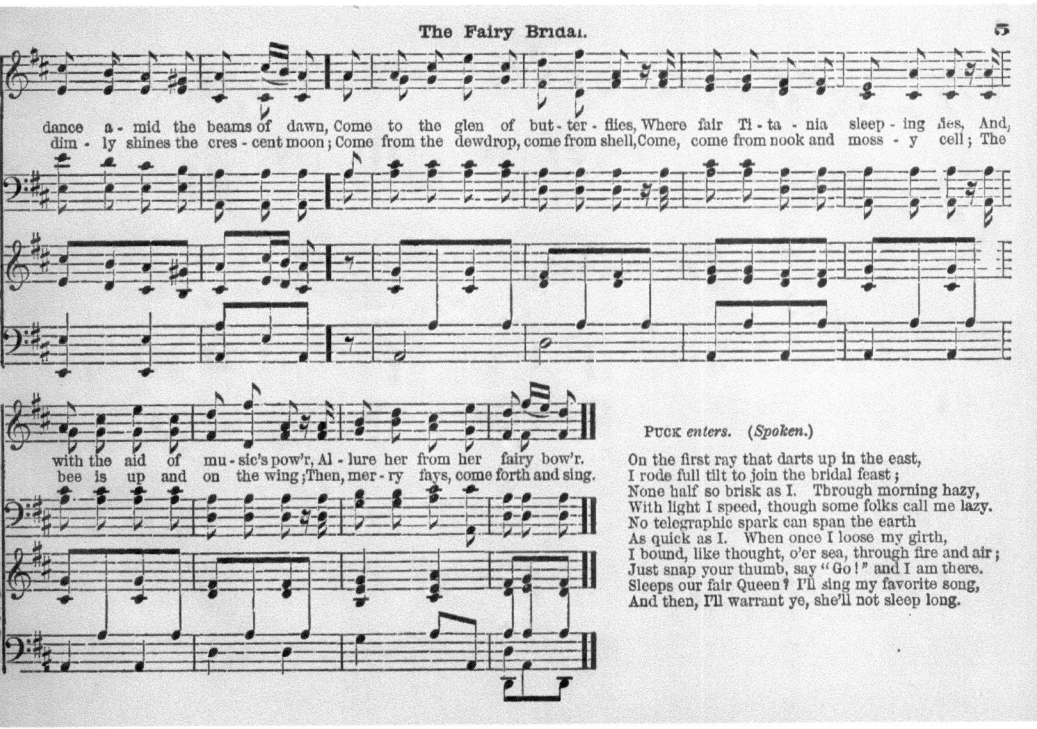

dance a - mid the beams of dawn, Come to the glen of but - ter - flies, Where fair Ti - ta - nia sleep - ing lies, And,
dim - ly shines the cres - cent moon; Come from the dewdrop, come from shell, Come, come from nook and moss - y cell; The

with the aid of mu - sic's pow'r, Al - lure her from her fairy bow'r.
bee is up and on the wing; Then, mer - ry fays, come forth and sing.

PUCK *enters.* (*Spoken.*)

On the first ray that darts up in the east,
I rode full tilt to join the bridal feast;
None half so brisk as I. Through morning hazy,
With light I speed, though some folks call me lazy.
No telegraphic spark can span the earth
As quick as I. When once I loose my girth,
I bound, like thought, o'er sea, through fire and air;
Just snap your thumb, say "Go!" and I am there.
Sleeps our fair Queen? I'll sing my favorite song,
And then, I'll warrant ye, she'll not sleep long.

The Fairy Bridal.

No. 2. *Solo.* Puck.

Allegretto.

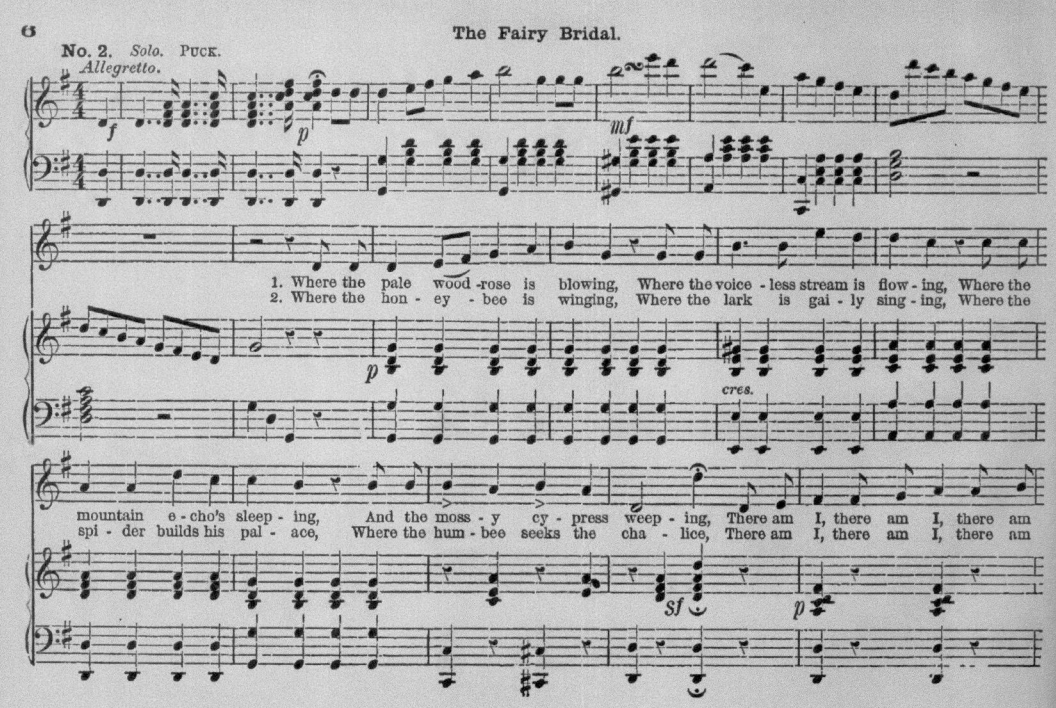

1. Where the pale wood-rose is blowing, Where the voice-less stream is flow-ing, Where the mountain e-cho's sleep-ing, And the moss-y cy-press weep-ing, There am I, there am I, there am

2. Where the hon-ey-bee is winging, Where the lark is gai-ly sing-ing, Where the spi-der builds his pal-ace, Where the hum-bee seeks the cha-lice, There am I, there am I, there am

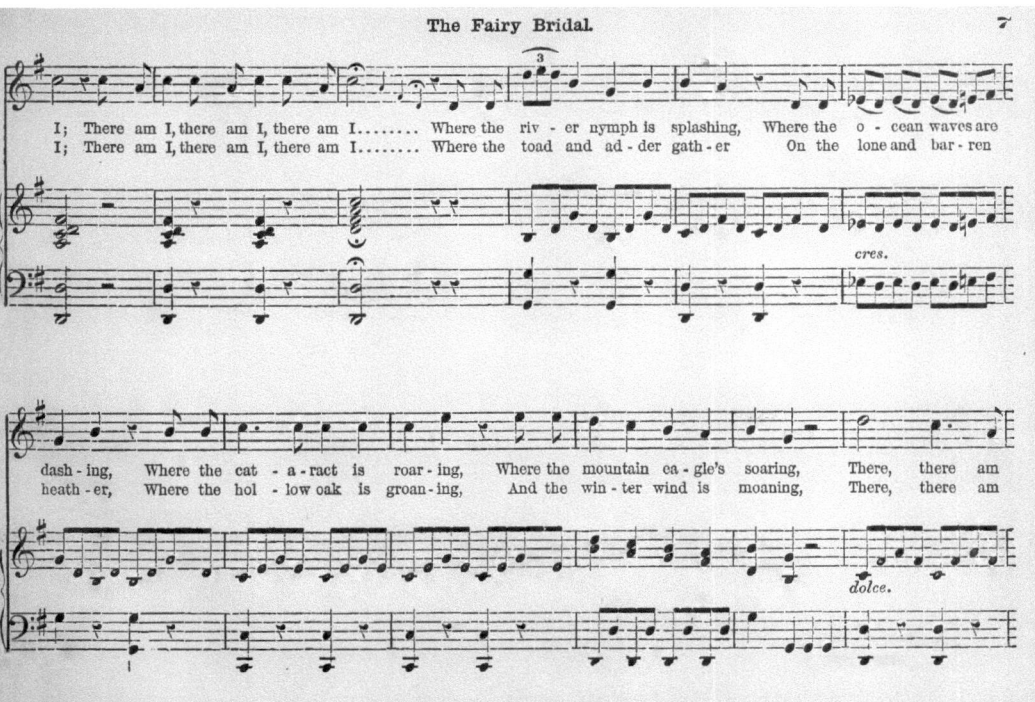

I; There am I, there am I, there am I........ Where the riv-er nymph is splashing, Where the o - cean waves are
I; There am I, there am I, there am I........ Where the toad and ad - der gath-er On the lone and bar-ren

cres.

dash - ing, Where the cat - a - ract is roar-ing, Where the mountain ea - gle's soaring, There, there am
heath - er, Where the hol - low oak is groan-ing, And the win - ter wind is moaning, There, there am

dolce.

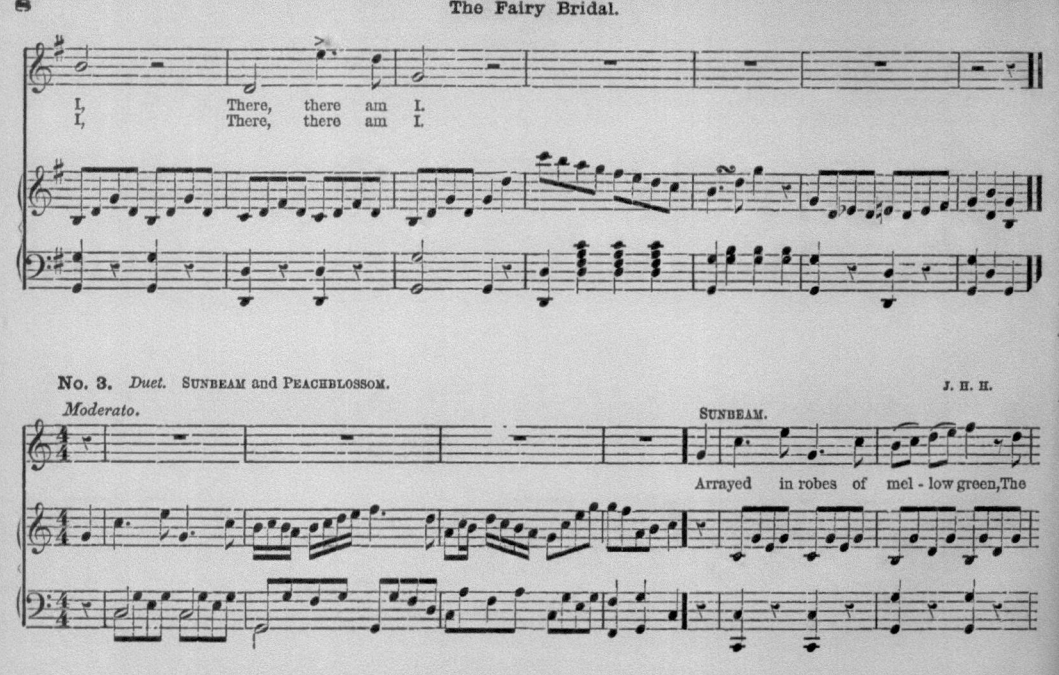

There, there am I.
There, there am I.

No. 3. *Duet.* SUNBEAM and PEACHBLOSSOM.

J. H. H.

Moderato.

SUNBEAM.

Arrayed in robes of mel - low green, The

for - est mon-arch rears his crest, To catch the flood of gold-en sheen That streams a - long the

cloudless east. How soft the mu - sic of the trees, How sweet the per-fume of the breeze! How

The Fairy Bridal.

soft the mu - sic of the trees, How sweet the per - fume of the breeze

PEACHBLOSSOM.

Our Fai - ry Queen comes with the light, Her voice is in the balm - y air; And all the hosts of

Duett.

accel.

in-sects bright, Proclaim her fair - est of the fair. The air is still, the bee - tle hums; Arrayed in light, she

f accel.

Chorus.

Enter TITANIA.

comes, she comes! Hail! all hail! Hail! all hail! Hail, all hail!

f

No. 4. *Solo.* TITANIA

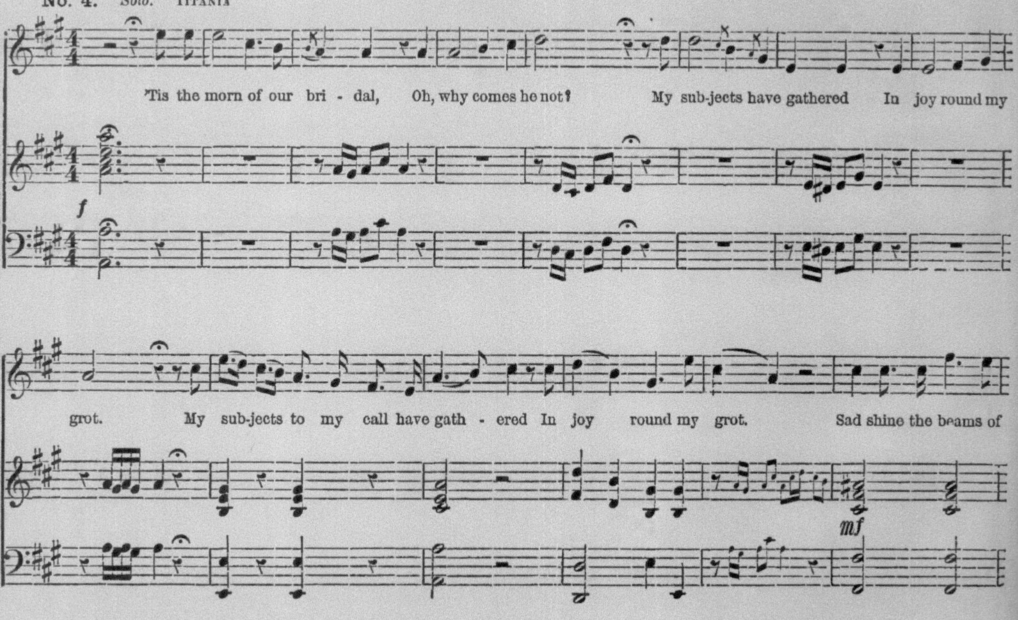

'Tis the morn of our bri - dal, Oh, why comes he not? My sub-jects have gathered In joy round my

grot. My sub-jects to my call have gath - ered In joy round my grot. Sad shine the beams of

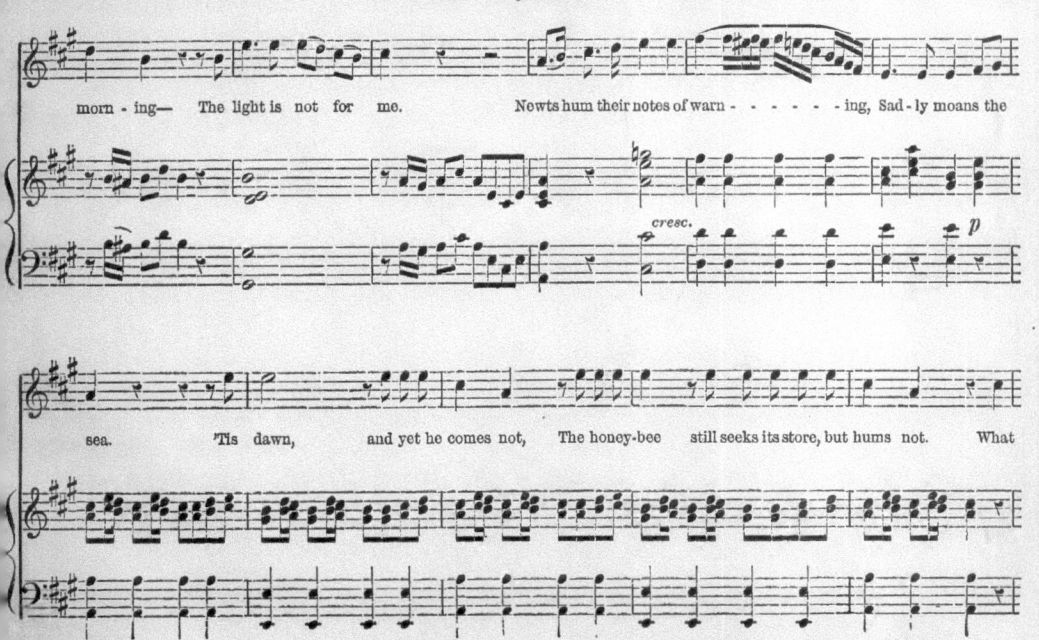

morn - ing— The light is not for me. Newts hum their notes of warn - - - - - ing, Sad - ly moans the

sea. 'Tis dawn, and yet he comes not, The honey-bee still seeks its store, but hums not. What

The Fairy Bridal.

signs are these? they bode me ill; When will my beat-ing heart be still? What signs are these? they bode me ill; When

will my heart be still? The crick - et now be - gins to sing; The woodland breeze is mur - mur - ing.

TITANIA.

I hear the crushing of the flow'rs, The song of sweet and playful hours, The song of sweet and play-ful hours. These sounds to me are

OBERON.

I come, fair Queen, with morning ray, When you command I must obey, When you command I must o-bey. These sounds to me are

notes of bliss, They fall up-on my heart Like dew up-on the drooping flow'r, That beams of noontide kiss. Love

The Fairy Bridal

love me? you love me? you say you love me?

I love thee, I love thee; Oh! shall I swear by

Yes, I am still thy fai-ry queen, Yes, I am still thy fai-ry queen. These sounds to me are

dew-drop sheen, That you are still my fai-ry queen? That you are still my fai-ry queen. These sounds to me are

The Fairy Bridal.

notes of bliss, They fall up - on my heart Like dew up - on the droop - ing flow'r That beams of noon-tide

kiss.   These sounds to me are notes   of bliss, They fall up - on my heart   Like dew up - on the

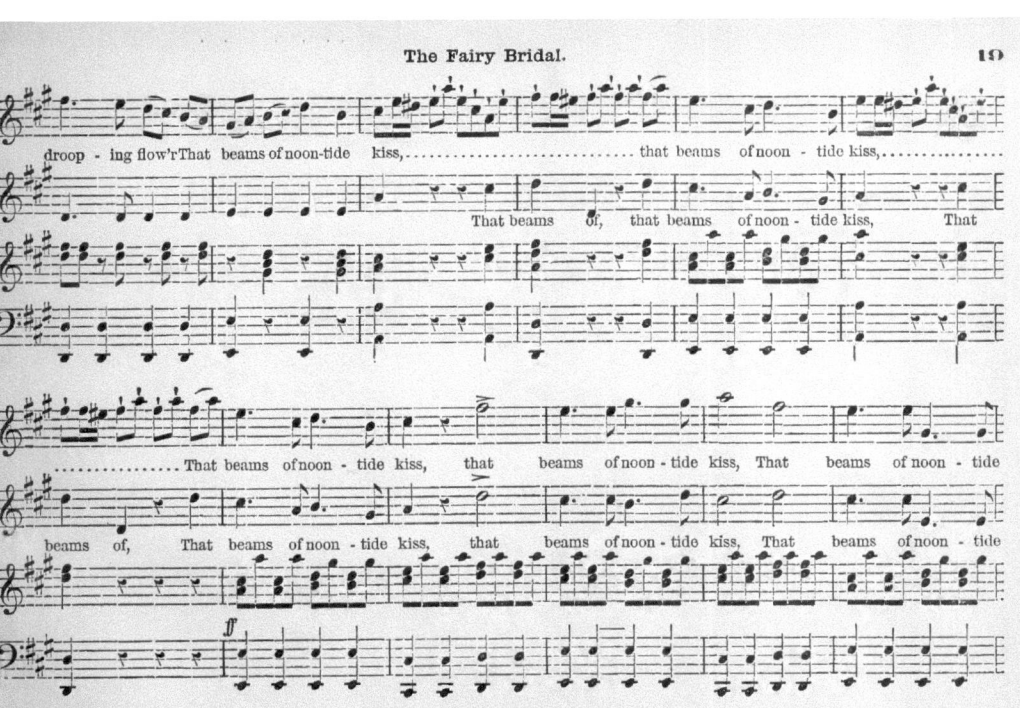

droop - ing flow'r That beams of noon-tide kiss,.............................. that beams of noon - tide kiss,...............

That beams of, that beams of noon - tide kiss, That

.... That beams of noon - tide kiss, that beams of noon - tide kiss, That beams of noon - tide

beams of, That beams of noon - tide kiss, that beams of noon - tide kiss, That beams of noon - tide

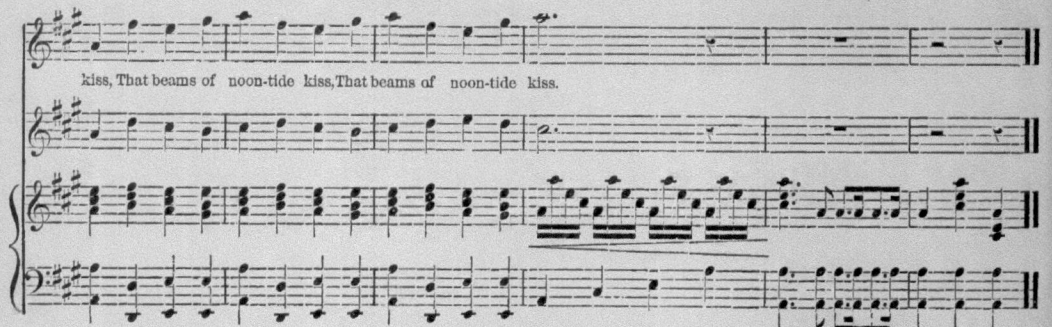

kiss, That beams of noon-tide kiss, That beams of noon-tide kiss.

TITANIA. (*Spoken.*)

Why did ye tarry? Love hath active wings;
Thine are the drone's, which to some heath-flower clings,
Sips its stale sweets, — then, passing slow along,
Sings to some other flow'r a whining song.
I'm angry with ye.

OBERON.

     Nay, my lovly Queen,
I hurried o'er the fields and meadows green
With lightning speed, and, thinking of thy smiles,
When, lo— a spider caught me in his toils.

In vain I strove to break the silken chain,
One pinion freed, its mate was bound again.
At length, a beetle broke my prison bars,
And I once more rose up toward the stars.

TITANIA.

'Tis well. The world is full of cunning traps,
To which fool-hardy men owe their mishaps;
We all spin webs to catch the foolish fly
That sports its gaudy wings while passing by.
I've spun *my* net—, and, round thee now I draw
The chain that binds thee to me evermore.

No. 5. TITANIA.

J. H. H.

Ho! all ye air - y things, Slaves of my will, Spread out your golden wings: The chalice fill.

SOPRANO AND ALTO.

1. Gath - er, gath - er round our lov'd rose, Ere the sun - beam warm - ly glows; Swift - ly,
2. Fleet - ly, fleet - ly from mos - sy bed, By the sound of mu - sic led; Gai - ly,

TENOR.

BASS.

The Fairy Bridal.

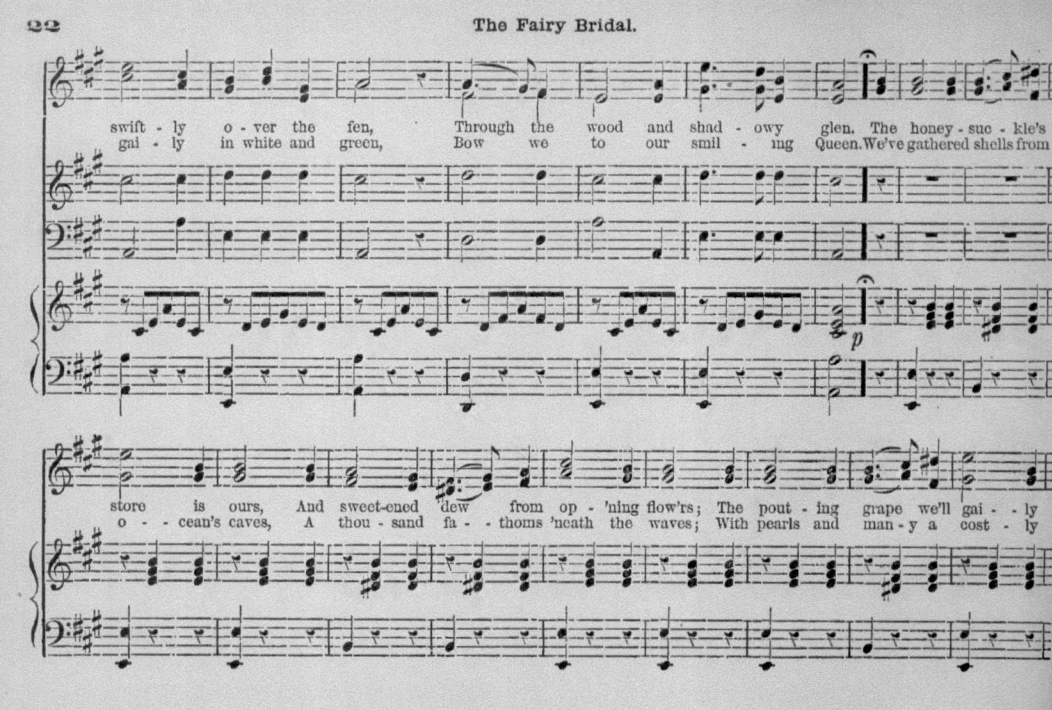

swift - ly   o - ver the   fen,   Through the   wood   and   shad - owy   glen. The honey - suc - kle's
gai - ly   in white and   green,   Bow   we   to   our   smil - ing   Queen. We've gathered shells from

store   is   ours,   And sweet-ened   dew   from op - 'ning flow'rs;   The pout - ing   grape we'll gai - ly
o - - cean's caves,   A   thou - sand   fa - - thoms 'neath the   waves;   With pearls and   man - y a   cost - ly

Enter Chorus of Gnomes.

squeeze, And pick sweet ber - - ries from the trees.
gem We'll deck Ti - ta - nia's di - - a - dem.

GNOME KING. (*Spoken.*)

Where mighty mountains tower above the vales,
In caverns deep, where toads and slimy snails
Crawl amid precious ores, we fairies dwell,
And make wild music for the forest dell.
We stir the fires that melt the golden ore
That makes men rich. Our lusty hammers roar
On the huge anvil, while we fashion things
That crush the poor and prop the power of kings
We come, O Queen, in rough, uncouth array,
At your command. Your slaves,—we must obey!

No. 6. *Solo.* BASS.

J. H. H.

1st.—Ten fath - oms
2d.—Here at your

Moderato.

p cres - - cen - - do *f* *f*

The Fairy Bridal.

deep   in rock - y mount,   Where bub - bles up   the la - va fount;   'Tis there we
bid - - - - ding, Fai - ry Queen,   We come from nook   and cav - ern green,   Where sli - my

p

2.   *Chorus.*

gnomes   our re - vels keep,   And stir the fires   in cav - erns deep.   Deep,   deep,   deep!
toad   and ad - der creep,   And thro' the cold,   cold win - ter sleep.   Sleep,   sleep,   sleep!

f

We've bars of gold, and sil-ver too, We've precious gems of ev-'ry hue; We sport and laugh in
Such moaning mu - - - sic as the cave Gives when the winds and wa-ters rave, Is all the song that

tasto.

dia - - mond cells, Where meteors burn and ech-o dwells. Dwells, dwells, dwells!
we can sing To make your fai - - - ry bow-er ring. Ring, ring, ring!

Chorus.

The Fairy Bridal.

VERDI.

1st.—See how bright the sparks are flashing, Hear the hammers thund'ring crashing, While the forge its red blaze free - ly yields.

2d.—Now the plowshare we are moulding, Now the rattling sheet un - fold - ing, Now we fashion swords and spears and shields.

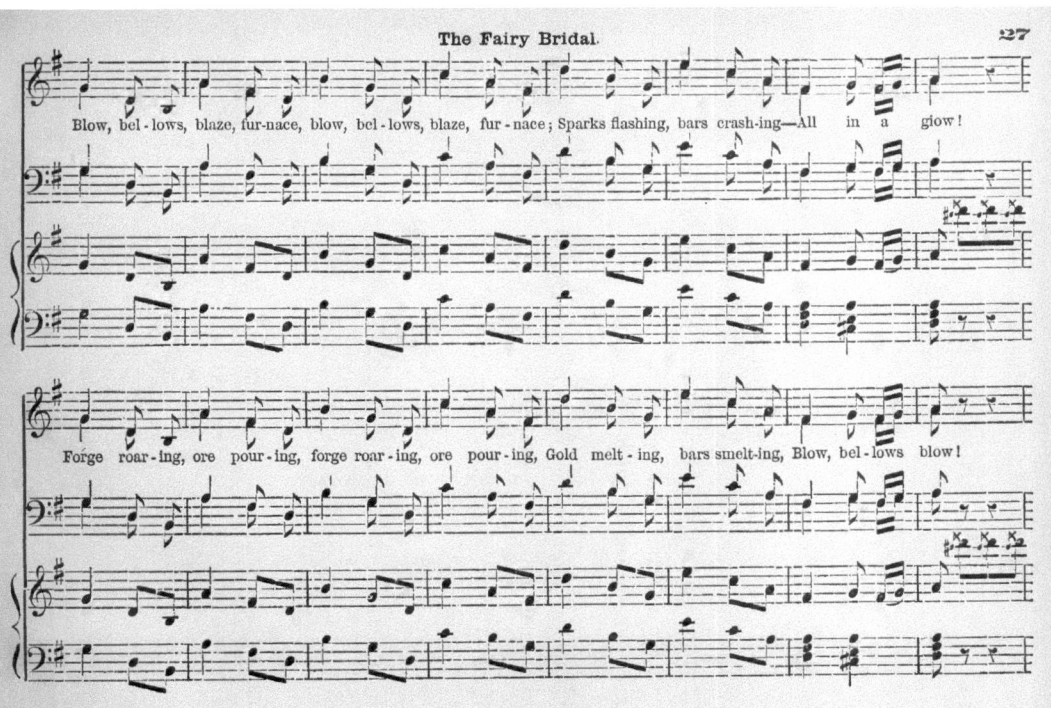

Blow, bel - lows, blaze, fur-nace, blow, bel - lows, blaze, fur - nace; Sparks flashing, bars crash-ing—All in a glow!

Forge roar - ing, ore pour - ing, forge roar - ing, ore pour - ing, Gold melt - ing, bars smelt-ing, Blow, bel - lows blow!

The Fairy Bridal.

Hail, gentle queen, we elf-ins, From our darksome home, Greet thee with song and chorus, Gladly we have come.

1st.—O - ver hill and o - ver mountain, Round the bush and round the fountain, Up the hill and down the dale, 'Mid
2d.—When the whip-poor-will is wail - ing, In a hol - low nut - shell sail - ing, O'er the glass - y stream we glide,

ro - ses red and lil - ies pale. Some-times on the bloom-ing heather, In the hon - ey - cup, we gather, When the bush is
With the fire - fly for our guide. In the lute, where mu - sic lin - gers, When untouched by mor - tal fingers, There we sleep, nor

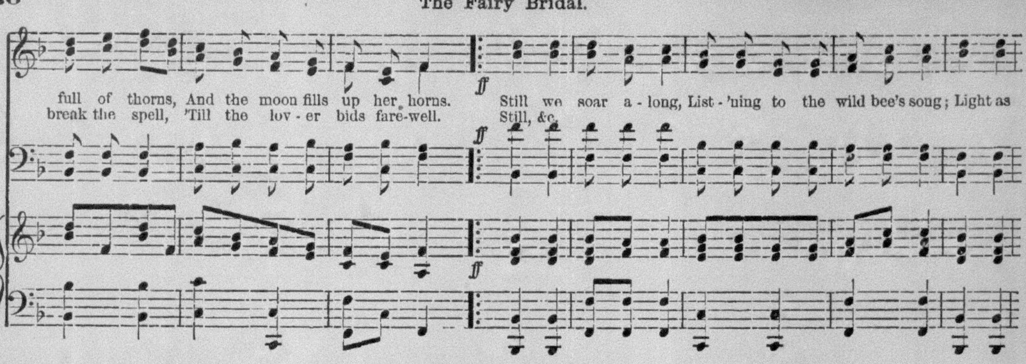

The Fairy Bridal.

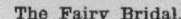

full of thorns, And the moon fills up her horns.
break the spell, 'Till the lov-er bids fare-well.

ff

Still we soar a-long, List-'ning to the wild bee's song; Light as
Still, &c.

snow-drops we, When they touch the wave-less sea.

SUNBEAM. (*Spoken.*)

Hail, beauteous Queen! hail, monarch of the woods!
From far and near, o'er wavy fields and floods,
The elfin host have come at your command,
A merry, sparkling, singing, fairy band.
Receive our homage, while the rites proceed,
Queen of the realm! lord of the hill and mead!

Andantino.

1. See her smil-ing as bright as the morn,　　When,
2. If to dream of one ob-ject a-lone,　　To

mf

p

cloudless, it glows in the sky;　　No dew-drop e'er slept 'neath a thorn,　　More pure in the rising sun's eye,　　More
treasure one name in the heart,　　Be loving, then I am thine own,　　And fond-ly be-lov-ed thou art,　　And

pure in the rising sun's eye.
fond- ly be- loved thou art.

Be
The

mine, fai- ry beau - ty, be mine! The treasures of earth, air, and sea, Command, and they all shall be
nee - dle that points to the pole, 'Tho' dark - ness o'er- shadow the sea, Was nev - er more true than the

Dolce.

thine, With the heart that is beating for thee; Yes, yes; with the heart that is beating for thee. ....
soul That swells in af - fec - tion for thee; Yes, yes; that swells in af - fec - tion for thee. ....

Rall.

No. 9. BRIDAL CHORUS. AUBER.

Bold.

Now the bri - dal rites be - ginning, Bring the wreath of spi - der's spinning, Twine it round her,

Solo.
fai - ry brow, And at the feet of beau - ty bow.
1st. Hail, Queen of beau - ty! We bend in
2d. Lord of the val - ley, Round thee we
du - ty To thy charms so daz - zling bright; Be ev - er
ral - ly; Be thou to her ten - der and true; Reign proud - ly

smil - ing, Sor - row be - guil - ing, Hap - py, gen - tle in.... thy might.
with her Hap - py to - geth - er, May each day thy joys re - new.

D.C.

D.C.

No. 10. *Solo.* TITANIA.
Recit.

J. H. H.

Ye elves and fai - ries of the wood profound, My slaves, in bright ar - ray,

come, gather 'round. Your Queen commands, her potent call o - bey. Her roy - al hands to love she yields to - day

Allegro non troppo.

Oh, joy - ful sounds of love a - wake, Let pleas - ure thrill thro' ev' - ry

bosom. The laugh and dance in bush and brake, A live-ly pulse in ev'-ry blossom. Shine out, O sun, thy golden

beams Give joy to ev'-ry liv-ing thing; While half the world is wrapp'd in dreams, Be ours the lot to dance and sing. We'll

The Fairy Bridal.

dance,   sing,   dance,   sing,   dance........ and   sing,   to dance and

Cres.   *f*

sing,   We'll   dance   and   sing, We'll dance, we'll dance and sing, We'll dance   and sing,

The Fairy Bridal.

CODA.*

Ah! .... Ah! ....

pp Swift, with air - y bound, Come, come, gather round; Swift, with air - y bound, Come, come, gather

Ah! ....

round. Swift, swift, swift, come gather round, Swift, Come, come gather round.

* This may be left out; if sung, it has the best effect without instrumental accompaniment.

No. 11. DANCING CHORUS.

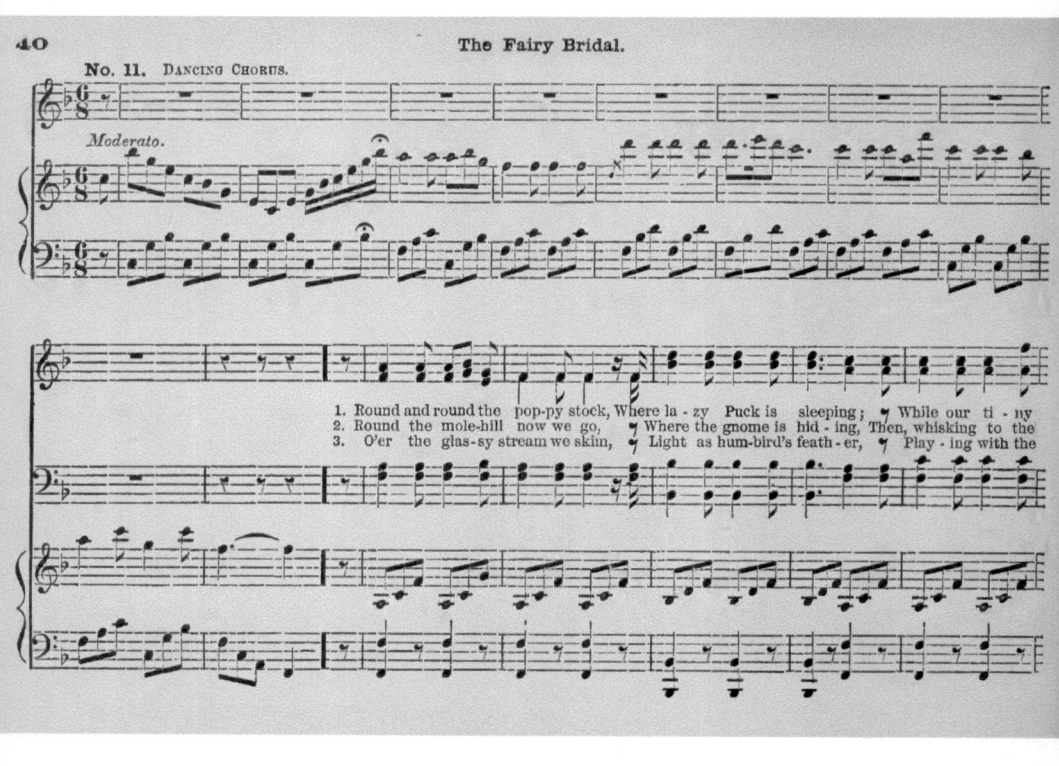

1. Round and round the pop-py stock, Where la - zy Puck is sleeping; While our ti - ny
2. Round the mole-hill now we go, Where the gnome is hid - ing, Then, whisking to the
3. O'er the glas-sy stream we skim, Light as hum-bird's feath - er, Play - ing with the

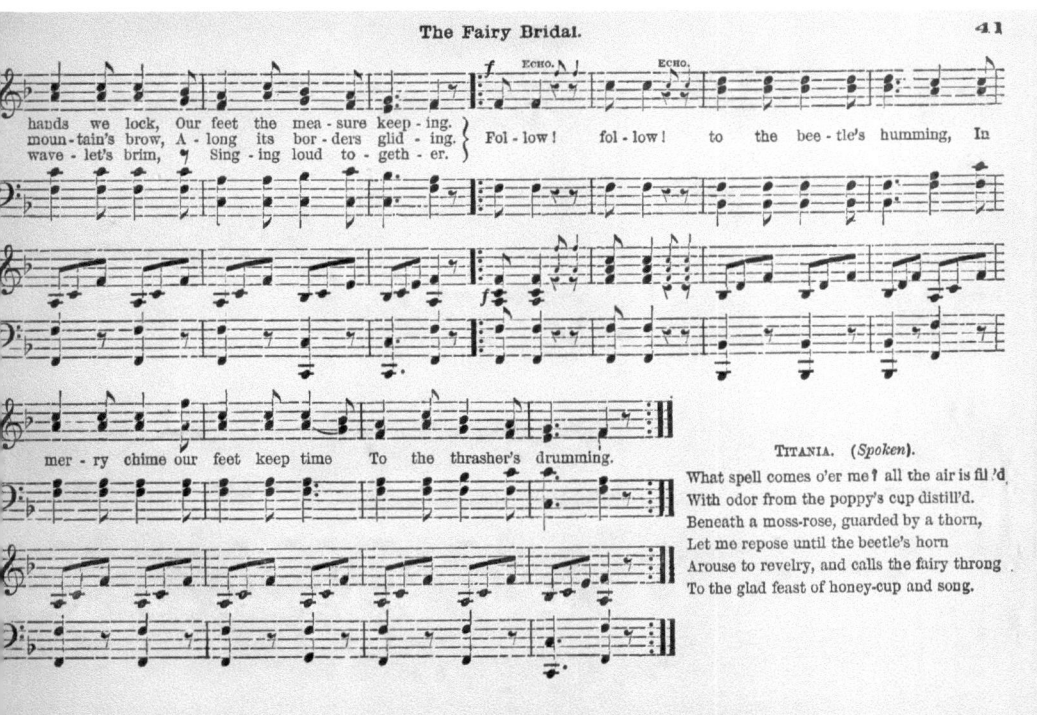

hands we lock, Our feet the mea-sure keep-ing.
moun-tain's brow, A - long its bor-ders glid-ing. } Fol-low! fol-low! to the bee-tle's humming, In
wave-let's brim, Sing-ing loud to-geth-er.

mer - ry chime our feet keep time To the thrasher's drumming.

TITANIA. (*Spoken*).

What spell comes o'er me? all the air is fil 'd
With odor from the poppy's cup distill'd.
Beneath a moss-rose, guarded by a thorn,
Let me repose until the beetle's horn
Arouse to revelry, and calls the fairy throng
To the glad feast of honey-cup and song.

The Fairy Bridal.

No. 12. *Trio.* OBERON, TITANIA, and PUCK.

Dew from the pop - py cup Falls on thine eyes; Sweet sleep comes o'er thee, With soft lul - la - - bies. TITANIA.—Un - der the rose - leaf,

There let me lie, Where cool zephyrs wan - der, And sing lul - la - - by.

mf

PUCK.

Breathe, softly breathe, ye be - ings of light, Break not her slum - bers, So fill'd with de -

The Fairy Bridal.

TITANIA. Sleep's creep - - ing on, dream of de - light,
OBERON. Sleep gent - - ly on, dream of de - light, 'Till the young stars gladden the night, Sleep gently
PUCK. - light.

on, dream of de - light, gent - ly sleep, gent - ly, gent - ly sleep. Sleep gently on, dream of de - light, gent - ly

The Fairy Bridal.

sleep, gent-ly, gent-ly sleep. Sleep gently on, gent-ly, gent-ly on. Sleep gent-ly on.

Sleep gently on, Sleep gent-ly on.

No. 13. *Chorus.*

J. H. H.

The morn is glowing in the east, Re-splendent up the cloud-less sky, The gol-den sunbeams

Lively.

The Fairy Bridal.

bright - ly dart, And lin - ger on the mountain high; The Fai - ry Queen, in slum - ber deep, Beneath a rose - leaf

shel - ter'd lies; Be noise - less, then, and let her sleep Be fill'd with dreams of me - lo - dies.

Duett. DEW-DROP AND STARLIGHT.

Down from the

Lento.

vi - o - let her pil - low forms,   An   a - corn cup her can - - - o - py;   The spi - der round her weaves his web, While

rall.

gnats   join   in   her lul - la - by. Gent - ly   slum - ber,   fair   Queen, Gent - ly   slum - ber, fair   Queen.

The Fairy Bridal.

Chorus *continued.*
Allegro.

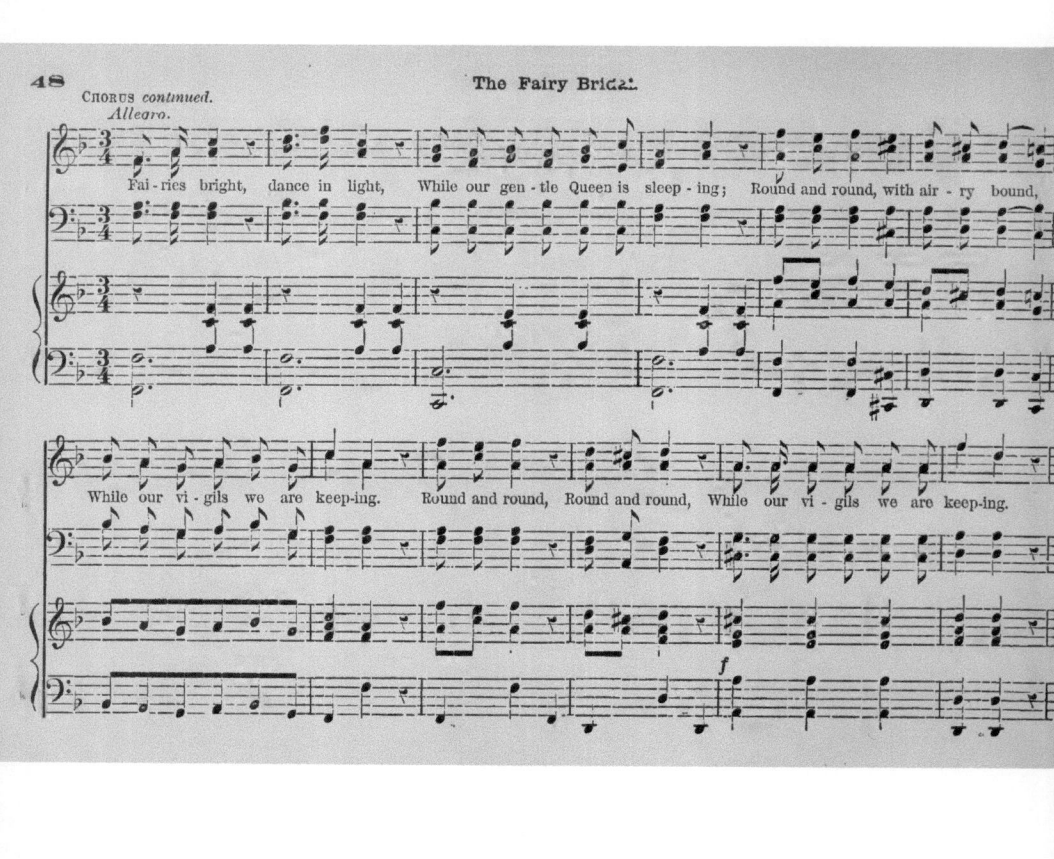

Fai-ries bright, dance in light, While our gen-tle Queen is sleep-ing; Round and round, with air-ry bound,

While our vi-gils we are keep-ing. Round and round, Round and round, While our vi-gils we are keep-ing.

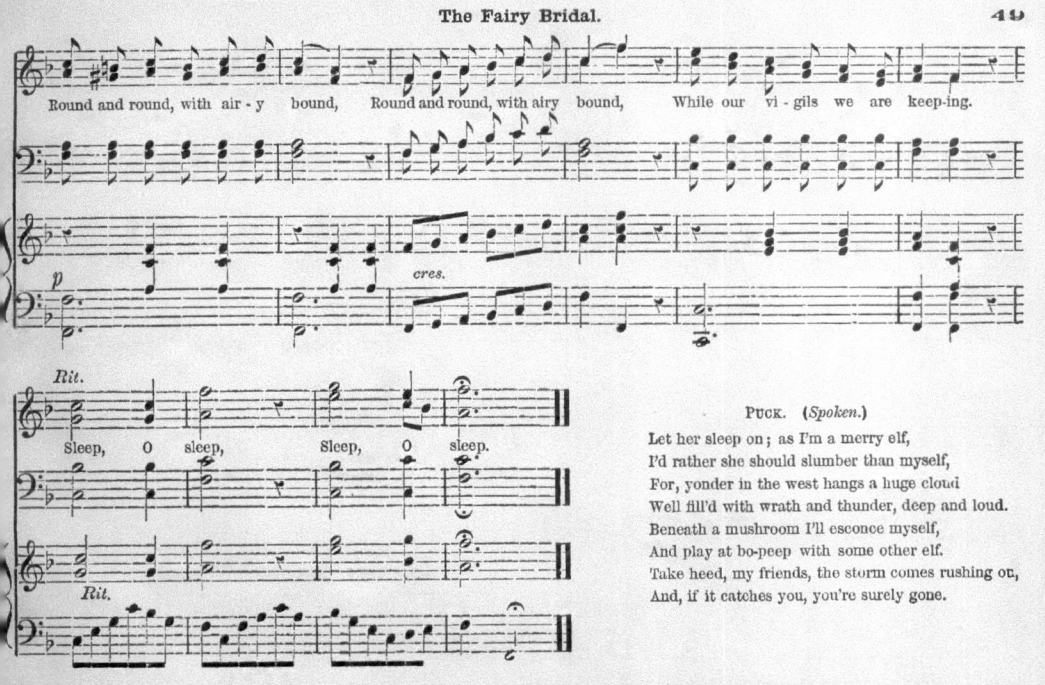

Round and round, with air - y bound, Round and round, with airy bound, While our vi - gils we are keep-ing.

p   *cres.*

Rit.

Sleep, O sleep, Sleep, O sleep.

Rit.

PUCK. (*Spoken.*)

Let her sleep on; as I'm a merry elf,
I'd rather she should slumber than myself,
For, yonder in the west hangs a huge cloud
Well fill'd with wrath and thunder, deep and loud.
Beneath a mushroom I'll esconce myself,
And play at bo-peep with some other elf.
Take heed, my friends, the storm comes rushing on,
And, if it catches you, you're surely gone.

No. 14. *Song of the* STORM FIEND.   J. H. H.

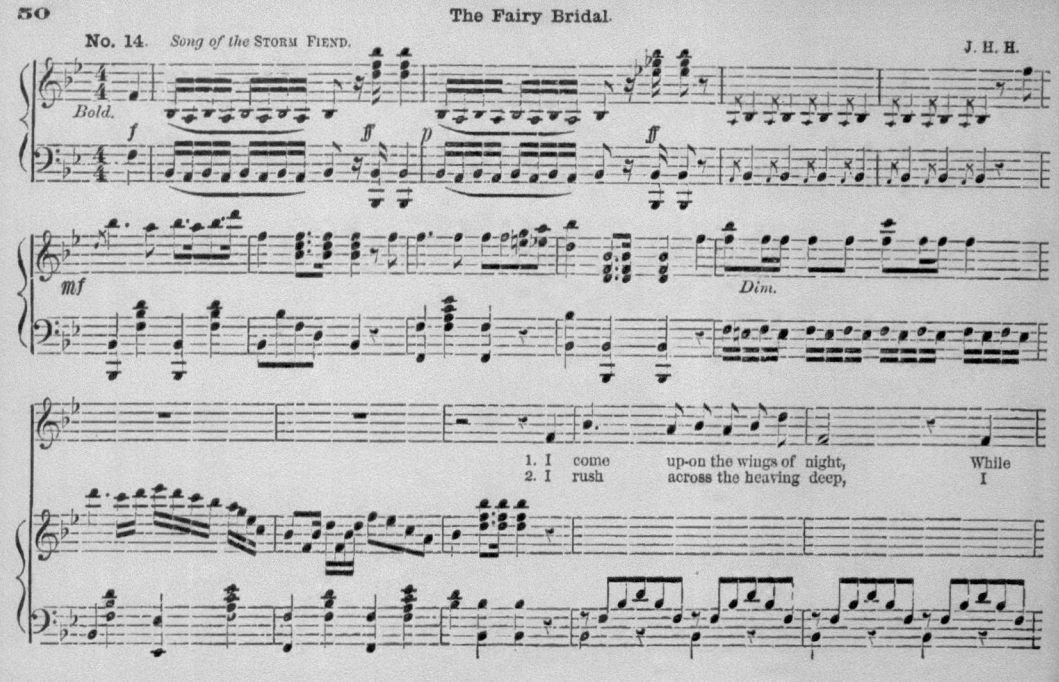

1. I   come   up-on the wings of night,   While
2. I   rush   across the heaving deep,   I

thun - - ders roll a - long my path, A - - round my brow are wreaths of light, That
rend the good ship's bending sails; I lull the mar - i - ner to sleep, And

cres.

shake their fie - ry shafts of wrath. The nois - y winds are pip - ing loud, The
laugh when - - e'er the bil - low wails; The gnarl - ed oak falls 'neath my pow'r, I

The Fairy Bridal.

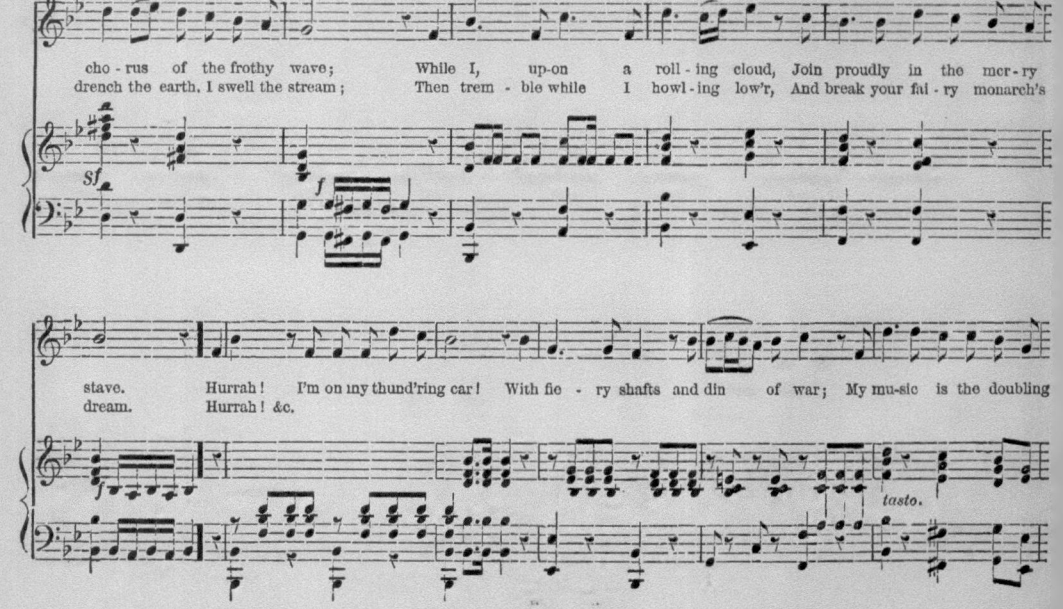

cho - rus of the frothy wave;   While I,   up-on   a   roll - ing cloud, Join proudly in the mer - ry
drench the earth, I swell the stream ;   Then trem - ble while   I   howl - ing low'r, And break your fai - ry monarch's

stave.   Hurrah !   I'm on my thund'ring car ! With fie - ry shafts and din   of war; My mu-sic is the doubling
dream.   Hurrah ! &c.

drum, Fly, while ye can, I come, I come!

No. 15. CHORUS.   J. H. H.

1 Hark!   to   the Storm Fiend's shout,   List   to   the wild wind's cry,   While roar - - ing an
2 See   ye   the flow'r-et's cup?   There   we'll   a   shel - ter   find;   From dan - - ger re-

The Fairy Bridal.

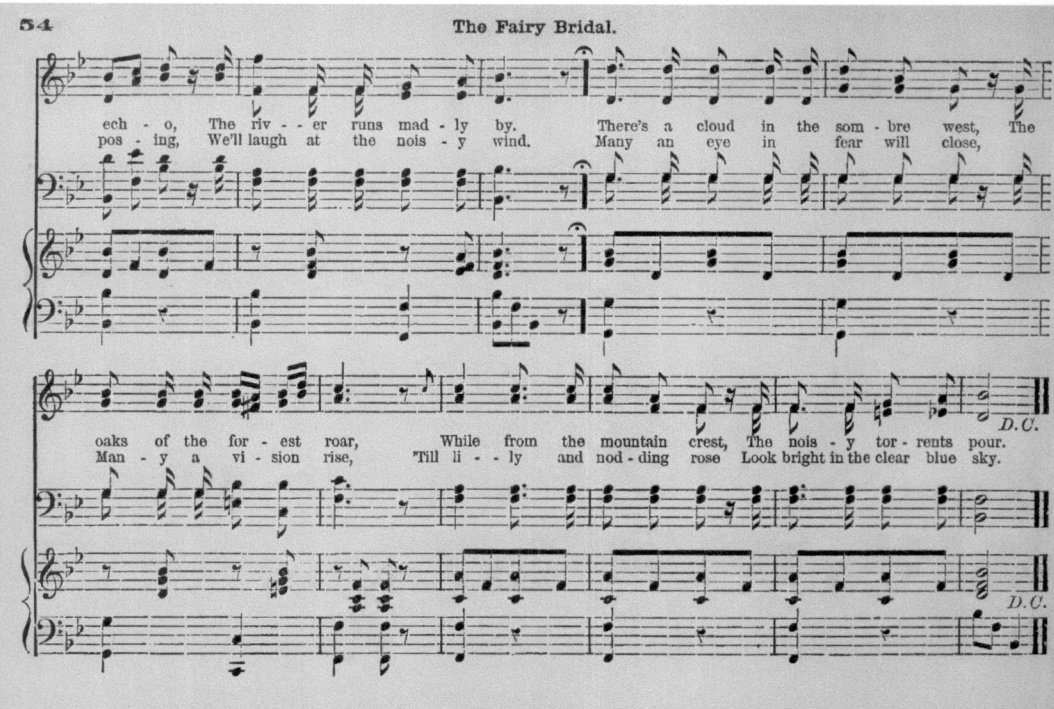

ech - o, The riv - er runs mad - ly by. There's a cloud in the som - bre west, The
pos - ing, We'll laugh at the nois - y wind. Many an eye in fear will close,

oaks of the for - est roar, While from the mountain crest, The nois - y tor - rents pour.
Man - y a vi - sion rise, 'Till li - ly and nod - ding rose Look bright in the clear blue sky.

D.C.

No. 16.

ROSSINI.

Oh, sweet the dream stole o'er me Of end - - less joys with

you,.......... Love danc'd in smiles be-fore me, And ev' - - ry bliss was new.

The Fairy Bridal.

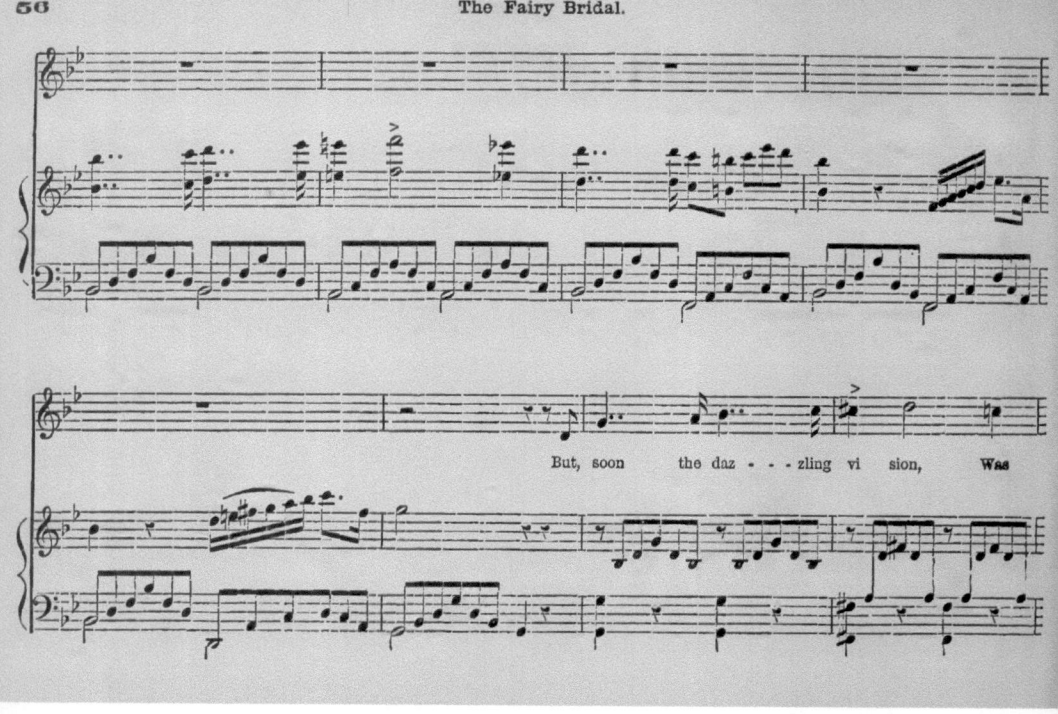

But, soon the daz - - -zling vi sion, Was

bro - - - ken—with - out   form,   The bow'rs   and fields   e - ly - - sian   Were

rav - - aged by   the   storm.

cres.

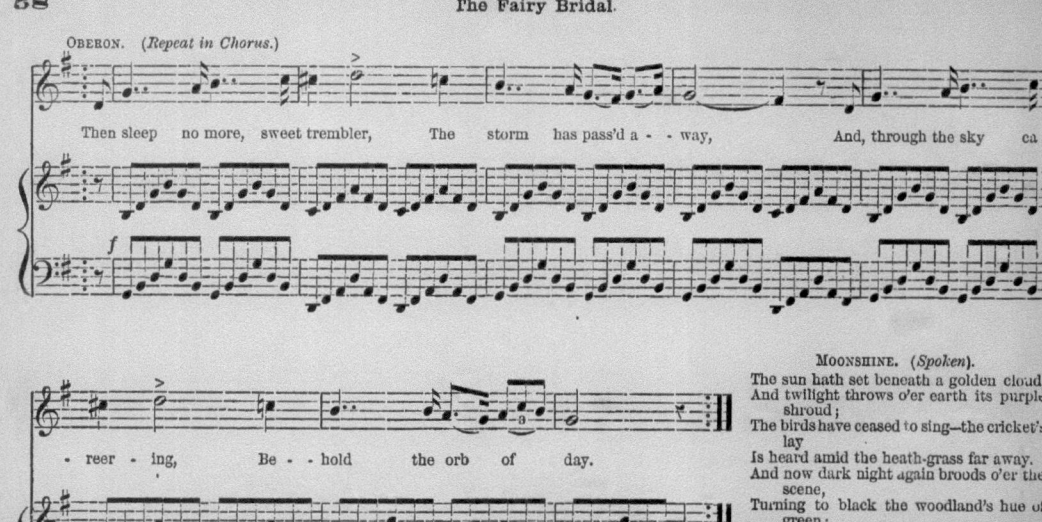

OBERON. (*Repeat in Chorus.*)

Then sleep no more, sweet trembler, The storm has pass'd a - - way, And, through the sky ca- - reer - ing, Be - - hold the orb of day.

MOONSHINE. (*Spoken*).

The sun hath set beneath a golden cloud,
And twilight throws o'er earth its purple
    shroud;
The birds have ceased to sing—the cricket's
    lay
Is heard amid the heath-grass far away.
And now dark night again broods o'er the
    scene,
Turning to black the woodland's hue of
    green;
And, lo! the moon, in all her majesty,
Rises above the mirror of the sea.
So pale, and yet so beautiful she looks
While looking down upon a thousand
    brooks.
Fairies, come forth and frolic in her light—
The earth's cold bride, the Princess of the
    night.

The Fairy Bridal.

No. 17. *Solo.* MOONSHINE.

J. H. H.

1 Twi-light sheds its glim'ring ray On mountain peak a - far,
2. Woods and dells are glooming fast, And birds have hush'd their song;

In the mist of dy-ing day, Be - hold the vesper star. Si - lent up the east-ern sky, Array'd in beams of
Far the mountain shadow's cast, So gloomy and so long. 'Tis the hour when fai - ries play; They love the pale and

The Fairy Bridal.

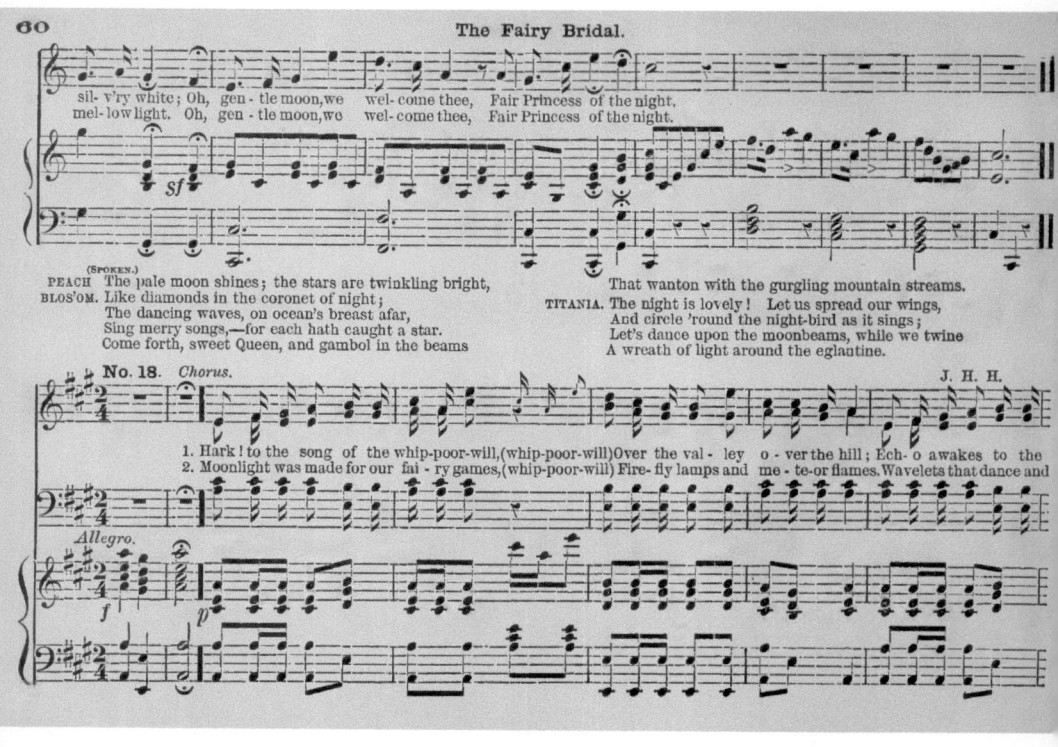

sil- v'ry white; Oh, gen - tle moon, we wel-come thee, Fair Princess of the night,
mel-low light. Oh, gen - tle moon, we wel-come thee, Fair Princess of the night.

sf

(SPOKEN.)

PEACH The pale moon shines; the stars are twinkling bright,
BLOS'OM. Like diamonds in the coronet of night;
The dancing waves, on ocean's breast afar,
Sing merry songs,—for each hath caught a star.
Come forth, sweet Queen, and gambol in the beams

That wanton with the gurgling mountain streams.

TITANIA. The night is lovely! Let us spread our wings,
And circle 'round the night-bird as it sings;
Let's dance upon the moonbeams, while we twine
A wreath of light around the eglantine.

No. 18. *Chorus.*

J. H. H.

1. Hark! to the song of the whip-poor-will,(whip-poor-will)Over the val - ley o - ver the hill; Ech- o awakes to the
2. Moonlight was made for our fai - ry games,(whip-poor-will) Fire- fly lamps and me - te-or flames.Wavelets that dance and

Allegro.

f   *p*

The Fairy Bridal.

doleful tune, (whip-poor-will) But we'll re-joice in the ris-ing moon. Trembling the glow-worm crawls a-long, And
sparkle bright, (whip-poor-will) And mock the gems of star-ry night. Un-der the leaf and prick-ly thorn, We'll

won-ders at our mer-ry song; Stern-ly the owl-et looks around, While 'hoot-ing at the jo-vial sound.
frol-ic a-way 'till ro-sy morn; And when the dew its sweets gives up, We'll slum-ber in the hon-ey cup.

DC

D.C.

No. 19.   *Solo*, ZEPHYR, and CHORUS.   J. H. H.

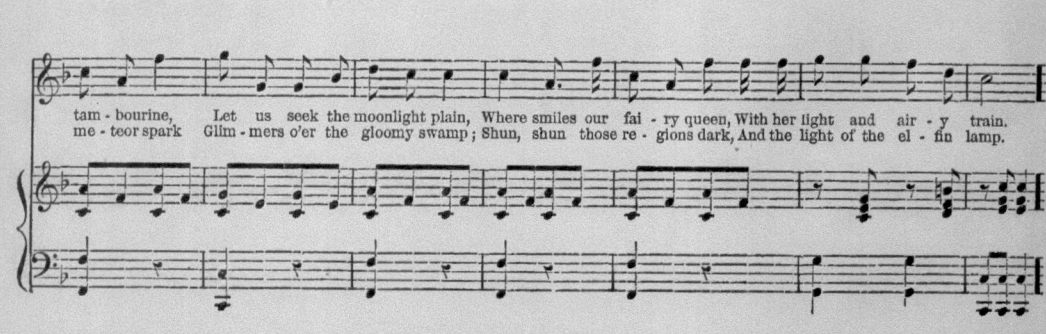

1. Sound, sound the
2. See, where the

tam - bourine,   Let us seek the moonlight plain, Where smiles our fai - ry queen, With her light and air - y train.
me - teor spark Glim - mers o'er the gloomy swamp; Shun, shun those re - gions dark, And the light of the el - fin lamp.

CHORUS.

Come, come, come, come, come, come, come, come, come, Where the sil - ver moonbeams play, Dance, dance, dance, dance, dance, dance, dance, dance,

f

SOLO.   CHORUS.   SOLO.   CHORUS.

Dance the merry hours a - way. Mer - ri - ly we'll gambol, Cheeri - ly we'll ramble Where the streamlet's flowing, And the lily's growing,
Where the faggot's blazing, Where the kine are grazing, Where the grass is growing, Where the cowslip's blowing,

cres.

The Fairy Bridal.

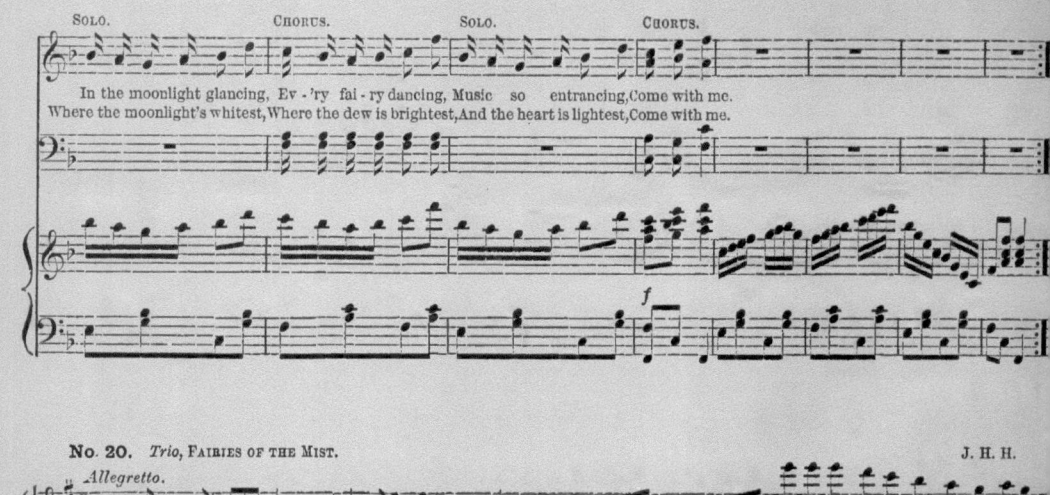

In the moonlight glancing, Ev-'ry fai-ry dancing, Music so entrancing,Come with me.
Where the moonlight's whitest, Where the dew is brightest,And the heart is lightest,Come with me.

No. 20. *Trio*, Fairies of the Mist. J. H. H.

The Fairy Bridal.

Trio. FAIRIES OF THE MIST.

J. H. H.

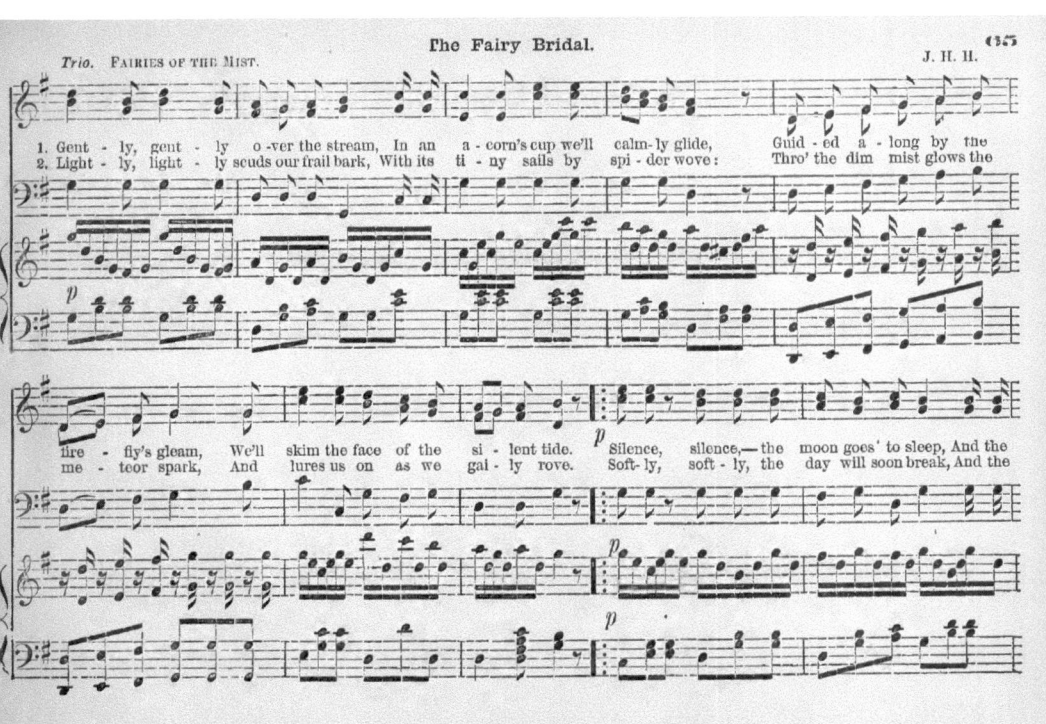

1. Gent - ly, gent - ly o - ver the stream, In an a - corn's cup we'll calm - ly glide, Guid - ed a - long by the
2. Light - ly, light - ly scuds our frail bark, With its ti - ny sails by spi - der wove: Thro' the dim mist glows the

fire - fly's gleam, We'll skim the face of the si - lent tide. Silence, silence,— the moon goes' to sleep, And the
me - teor spark, And lures us on as we gai - ly rove. Soft- ly, soft - ly, the day will soon break, And the

The Fairy Bridal.

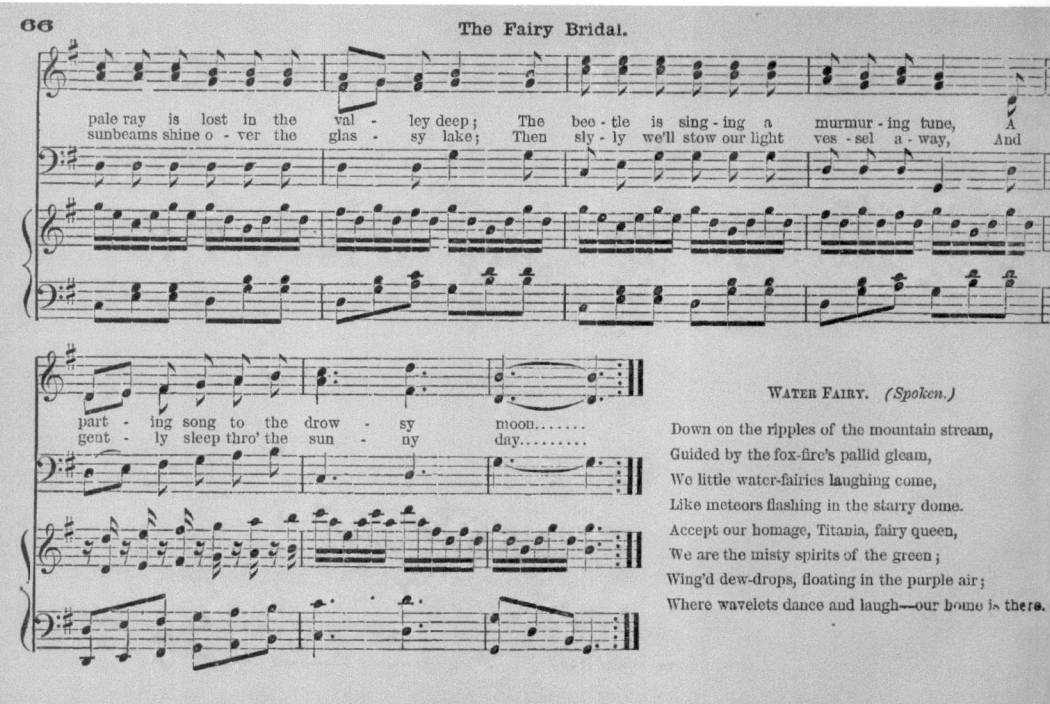

pale ray is lost in the val - ley deep; The bee - tle is sing - ing a murmur - ing tune, A
sunbeams shine o - ver the glas - sy lake; Then sly - ly we'll stow our light ves - sel a - way, And

part - ing song to the drow - sy moon.......
gent - ly sleep thro' the sun - ny day.........

WATER FAIRY. *(Spoken.)*

Down on the ripples of the mountain stream,
Guided by the fox-fire's pallid gleam,
We little water-fairies laughing come,
Like meteors flashing in the starry dome.
Accept our homage, Titania, fairy queen,
We are the misty spirits of the green;
Wing'd dew-drops, floating in the purple air;
Where wavelets dance and laugh—our home is there.

The Fairy Bridal.

No. 21. CHORUS OF WATER-FAIRIES. *Sung by little girls.* J. H. H.

SOPRANO AND ALTO.

Allegro.

1. Where the gush-ing wa-ters flow, Kiss-ing flow'rets as they go, Gent-ly, sly-ly stealing on,
2. Where the spray is dashing high, To the cat-'ract's melo-dy, And the bil-lows wild-ly roar

Hid-den from the noonday's sun. There you'll find us merri-merri-ly, Pret-ty wa-ter-fai-ries we,
On the dark and rock-y shore,

There you'll find us, merri-merri-ly, Pret-ty wa-ter-fairies we.

TITANIA. *(Spoken.) (To the audience.)*

And now the veil upon the scene must fall;
Fairies no more, we bid farewell to all.
'Twas but a dream—a glimpse at fairy-land,
Where dancing elves sport gaily, hand in hand.
The vision's past, and hushed the magic strain
That fill'd the air—we've come to earth again.
If sounds discordant reach'd your tutor'd ear,
Do not condemn with judgment too severe;
We're not proficients, but we thought our song,
Though juvenile, might please the list'ning throng.

The Fairy Bridal.

No. 22 TITANIA, OBERON, AND CHORUS.

J. H. H.

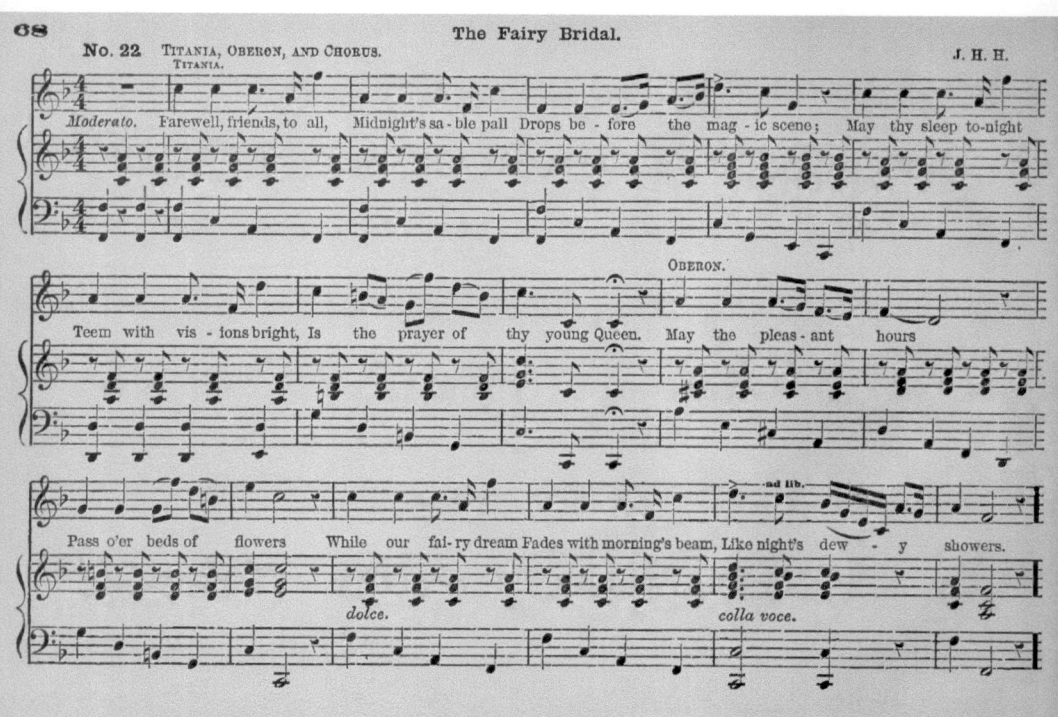

Moderato. Farewell, friends, to all, Midnight's sa - ble pall Drops be - fore the mag - ic scene; May thy sleep to-night

Teem with vis - ions bright, Is the prayer of thy young Queen. May the pleas - ant hours

Pass o'er beds of flowers While our fai - ry dream Fades with morning's beam, Like night's dew - y showers.

The Fairy Bridal.

DUET. TITANIA AND OBERON.

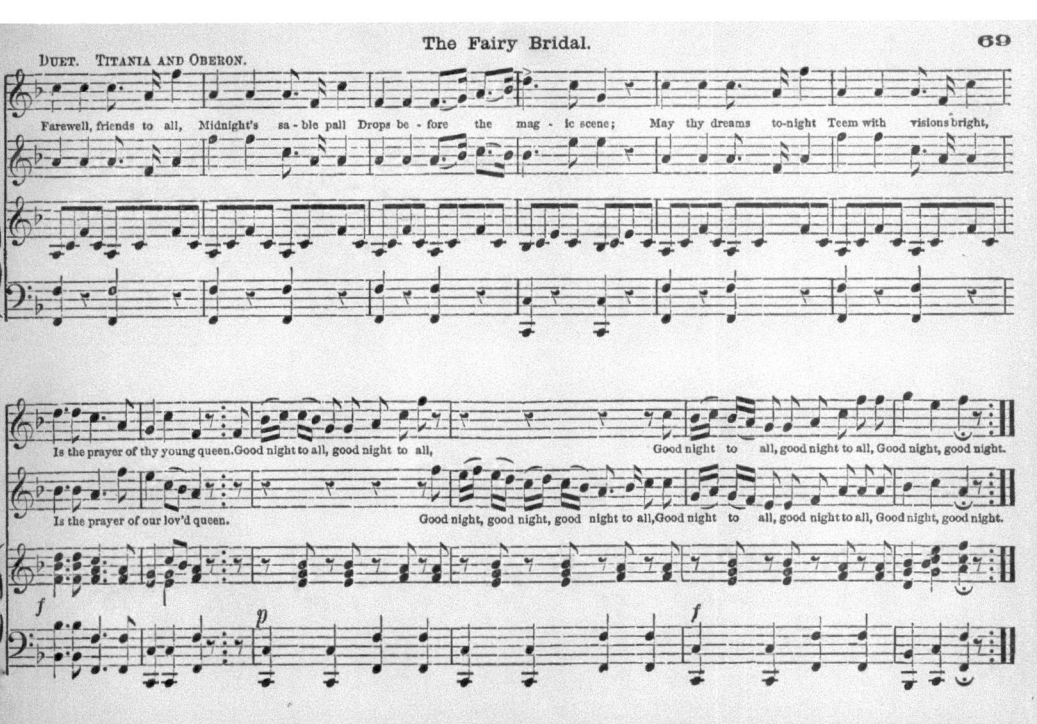

Farewell, friends to all, Midnight's sa - ble pall Drops be - fore the mag - ic scene; May thy dreams to-night Teem with visions bright,

Is the prayer of thy young queen. Good night to all, good night to all, Good night to all, good night to all, Good night, good night.

Is the prayer of our lov'd queen. Good night, good night, good night to all, Good night to all, good night to all, Good night, good night.

No. 23. FINALE

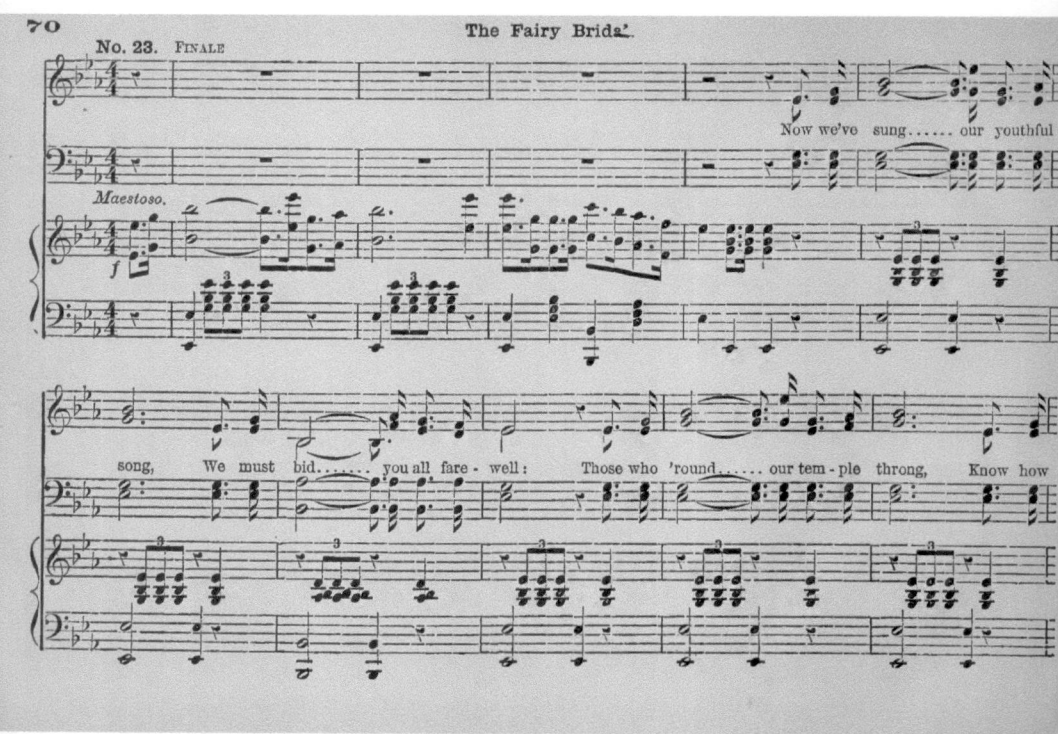

Now we've sung...... our youthful

song,   We must bid...... you all fare-well: Those who 'round...... our tem-ple throng,   Know how

The Fairy Bridal.

The Fairy Bridal.

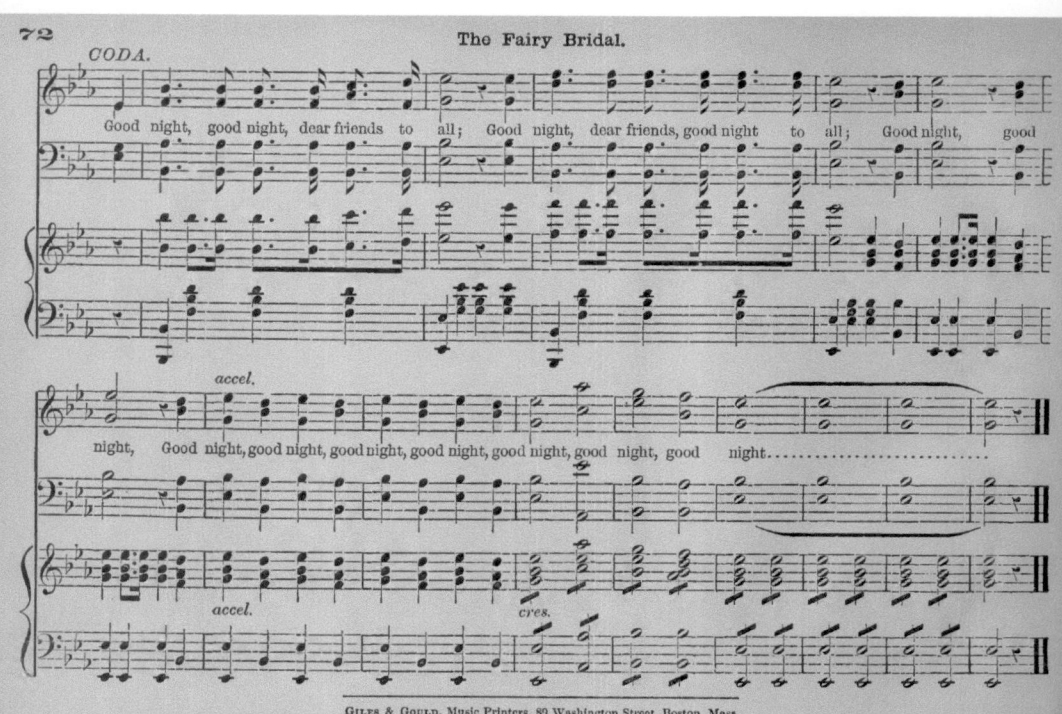

CODA.

Good night, good night, dear friends to all; Good night, dear friends, good night to all; Good night, good

night, Good night, good night, good night, good night, good night, good night, good night.......................

accel.

accel.   *cres.*

GILES & GOULD, Music Printers, 89 Washington Street, Boston, Mass

CHORUS AND GLEE BOOKS FOR CHORUS CHOIRS AND SINGING SCHOOLS.

PERKINS' GLEE AND CHORUS BOOK. By H. S. PERKINS.

This is a thoroughly goo collection of Choruses, Anthems, Glees and Part-Songs, gathered from the latest and best books of the best composers. Price........$1.25.

THE CHORUS CHOIR. By E. TOURJÉE.

A collection of Anthems, Motets, Chants, etc., highly commended, and selected from the works of the ablest composers. Price........................$1.50.

FESTIVAL CHORUS BOOK. By J. P. COBB.

A collection of Anthems, Choruses and Part-Songs, which have been tried and proved successful, and gives an abundance of good music in every way adapted for festivals, conventions, singing schools, or, indeed, for any chorus. Price......$1.25.

PERKINS' ANTHEM BOOK. By W. O. PERKINS.

A fine collection of Anthems for Sunday service, as well as for general use by societies. All the selections are fresh and interesting, with easy music. Price, $1.50.

AMERICAN GLEE BOOK. By W. O. PERKINS.

A true glee book of recent publication, and containing all the newest and best Glees, adapted to the wants of glee clubs and choruses. Price................$1.50.

GERMAN FOUR-PART SONGS. Compiled by N. H. ALLEN.

These Glees or Songs are from the best works of the more modern German writers, are very bright and lively, have the English words, and are for mixed voices. Price ....$1.50.

THE ANTHEM HARP. By W. O. PERKINS.

This book contains about eighty Anthems and twenty Chants and Responses, suitable for all occasions where the singing of Anthems and set pieces is required. Price..$1.25.

AMERICAN ANTHEM BOOK. By JOHNSON, TENNEY and ABBEY.

This book has Anthems for general service, for special occasions, for practice, and for public singing, especially arranged for chorus choirs. The compilers have been most fortunate in their selections and compositions, most of which are by the authors. Price..$1.25.

EMERSON'S CHORUS BOOK. By L. O. EMERSON.

The Choruses and Glees in this book have been chosen with the author's usual good taste, and are excellently adapted for use by musical societies and singing schools generally. Price..$1.25.

EMERSON'S ANTHEM BOOK. By L. O. EMERSON.

A new anthem book with a great variety of new music for opening and closing of service. There are over one hundred Anthems, Chants and Responses. $1.25.

THE PEOPLE'S CHORUS BOOK.

Secular Choruses and four-part Songs for mixed voices. It is of medium size and contains about thirty selections of the best quality. Price................$1.00.

THE GEM GLEANER. By J. M. CHADWICK.

A collection of Anthems with easy music, which has been tested, and will prove very serviceable for general society practice. Price........................$1.00.

THE CHORUS WREATH.

Sacred and secular Choruses, selected from the best oratorios, operas and glee books, most of which have been used in the great Jubilee, and sung at all the popular musical conventions and festivals. Price........................$1.50.

Very choice collections of Glees, Part-Songs and Choruses will be found in the newer Church Music books and books for Singing Schools.

☞ Any of the above books mailed, post-paid, for the price named.

BOSTON:
OLIVER DITSON COMPANY.

| *NEW YORK:* | *CHICAGO:* | *PHILADELPHIA:* | *BOSTON:* |
| C. H. DITSON & CO. | LYON & HEALY. | J. E. DITSON & CO. | JOHN C. HAYNES & CO |